WHY
STARS COME OUT AT NIGHT

Written by Eric Pullin
Illustrated by Chris Davis
(Student at Stevenson College Edinburgh)

WHY STARS COME OUT AT NIGHT
copyright 2009 Eric Pullin

ISBN No: 978.1.906542.19.1
First published 2009

Publishers: Barny Books, Hough on the Hill
Grantham, Lincolnshire, NG32 2BB

Tel: 01400 250246   www.barnybooks.biz

Printed by Minuteman Press, Edinburgh, Scotland
Tel: 0131 444 0800

Dear Reader,

MR BARNY OWL FROM OUR FIRST STORY HAS GOT LOST

Although I've hunted everywhere
I can't find Owl – he isn't there.
He must be hiding in this book
So please be kind and take a look
And if you spot him write to me
I might just send you something FREE

Where's Barny? Write to eric.pullin@tiscali.co.uk and tell me.

Visit our website at www.thewhyseries.co.uk

I wonder if you've ever tried
To count the stars up in the sky
And if you have I'm sure you've found
Your head began to spin around.
So many stars all shining bright -
But why do they come out at night?

It helps to know what stars are for

And why there should be stars at all

And where they go to when the sun

Comes up and shines on everyone.

Now, if you listen carefully

We'll try to solve this mystery.

There is a country, very cold,

Where lives a man who's very old.

A kind old man who never sleeps.

All day and night this old man keeps

An eye on every newborn child,

And for each one the old man smiles.

9

The old man smiles because he knows

He's work to do - so off he goes

To where the snow lies thick and white

For he must find some snow just right

To make the gift he has in mind

And perfect snow is hard to find.

10

He takes his shiny silver spade

Together with a bucket made

From pieces of the finest gold

Which keeps the snow he carries cold

So it won't melt on his way home,

Then back he hurries all alone.

Back at his house the old man breaks

The snow up into tiny flakes,

Then every flake he checks with care

And picks the best ones that are there.

Guess what - the flakes he chooses are

The ones shaped like a perfect star.

The old man then takes out his list
Of babies born - none must be missed.
Although each snow star looks the same
He gives each one a new child's name
And then he casts a magic spell,
The words of which he'll never tell.

To every star so pure and white

He fits a small electric light.

He takes a bulb and batteries too

And sticks them on with super glue.

Then once again he checks the list

To make quite sure no name's been missed.

Glue

Emily
Matthew
Hannah
Christopher
Ashley
Nicolas
Sarah
Michael
Jessica

The old man's work is never done

He has a star for everyone

But now the time has come to fly

And take them way up in the sky

To find each one the perfect place

Where it can shine on baby's face.

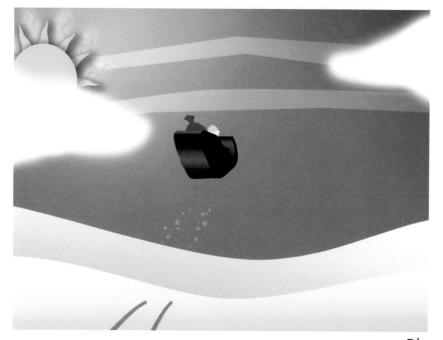

So on his magic sleigh he rides
Up through the clouds into the skies.
He takes a hammer and some nails
And plasters - 'cause he never fails
To hit his thumb when trying to knock
A nail into the perfect spot.

23

On every nail he hangs a star

To shine on baby from afar.

He sets the switch to make the light

Come on when day turns into night

But still his work is not quite done,

"Don't go down yet!" he tells the sun.

Day Night

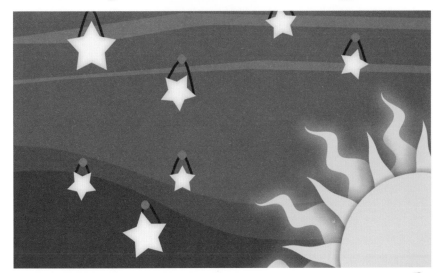

25

The brand new stars are all in place
So now it's time for him to race
To every other star around
And check for batteries running down.
It simply wouldn't be quite right
For any star to lose its light.

All batteries checked, back home he goes.

He's kept so busy I suppose

He hasn't even time to yawn

Before the next new baby's born.

He'll have a brand new star to make.

No time for him to take a break.

Jacob ⬭
Emma ⬭
Joshua ⬭
Madison ⬭
Ethan ⬭
Olivia ⬭
Daniel ⬭
Samantha ⬭
Joseph ⬭
Sophia ⬭
William ⬭
Grace ⬭
Ryan ⬭
Natalie ⬭

29

So, now you know what stars are for

And why we just see more and more,

It's time to tell you why it's right

That stars should twinkle just at night.

The reason is a simple one,

It's all to do with Mr. Sun.

All day long the sun shines down

And smiles on everyone around

And just for luck you've grown-ups who

Are there to keep an eye on you,

But who will be around to keep

You safe when grown-ups are asleep?

That's right - you have a special star
Who knows exactly where you are
And watches you from far away
To keep you safe 'til break of day -
But he can't shine the whole day round
For that would run his batteries down!

Author's note

Writing "The Why Series" is easy. The difficult part is getting the stories from inside my head to in front of your eyes and there are many people that I would like to thank for the help that they have given me in doing this.

Chris, my brilliant illustrator. Jayne and Molly at my publishers, Barny Books. Richard and the staff at Minuteman Press, my printers. Marjory and Ronnie and the students at Stevenson College Edinburgh. Special thanks to my wife Penny and my sister Gill together with the rest of my family for their constant encouragement and support.

Last but not least my beautiful grand daughters Lucy and Lulah for whom these stories were originally written.
I am indebted to you all.

www.thewhyseries.co.uk